Read-Along
STORYBOOK AND CD

Luca, a sea monster boy, meets an unexpected friend. Together they experience an unforgettable summer in a human town. To find out what happens, read along with me in your book. You will know it is time to turn the page when you hear this sound. . . . Let's begin now.

Published by Disney Press, an imprint of Buena Vista Books, Inc. No part of this book may be reproduced or transmitted in any form or by any means, electronic or mechanical, including photocopying, recording, or by any information storage and retrieval system, without written permission from the publisher. For information address Disney Press, 1200 Grand Central Avenue, Glendale, California 91201.

Printed in the United States of America

First Paperback Edition, May 2021   10 9 8 7 6 5 4 3 2 1

Library of Congress Control Number: 2020949946

FAC-009121-21085

ISBN 978-1-368-06708-9

For more Disney Press fun, visit www.disneybooks.com

Disney PRESS
Los Angeles • New York

Ever since he was a young sea monster, Luca Paguro had wondered what lay beyond the surface of the water. It was always there, shimmering and rippling, just above his head. Yet no matter how much he wanted to, Luca never explored it, for a different kind of monster lived up there. *Land monsters*. Humans, to be exact, who hunted sea-folk with boats and harpoons. Luca was forbidden by his parents to go anywhere near the surface.

One morning, with his flock of goatfish, Luca stumbled across some strange items. Then, suddenly, a masked land monster appeared! Luca tried to escape but found himself cornered. The land monster advanced, brandishing a harpoon. But instead of throwing it, the creature pulled off its mask, revealing an older sea monster boy. "It's fine. I'm not human."

Luca was relieved but concerned. Then the boy explained that he was there for his stuff, and he took Luca's shepherd's crook.

"Wait! That's mine!" Luca chased the boy toward the sunlight . . .

. . . and right through the surface! Luca gasped when he realized where he was. Then something amazing happened. His webs became fingers. His scales became skin. His tail disappeared completely!

The older boy, whose name was Alberto, explained that whenever sea monsters leave the water, their bodies transform to look like humans. Whenever they get wet again, they go back to their sea monster selves.

Alberto's home was an island hideout. He said he lived with his dad, who let him do whatever he wanted. Luca gazed at all his items, stopping on a poster. "What's that?"

Alberto's eyes gleamed. "Oh, it's just the greatest thing that humans ever made. The Vespa."

Luca looked around again. "Are you gonna make one? I think you have all the parts."

Alberto grew excited. He had never considered building one. The boys immediately got to work. Hours later, they had made their own makeshift Vespa.

When Luca sat down at the dinner table that evening, his family was worried. He had been out much later than usual. Luckily, his grandmother covered for him, saying that she had sent him to look for sea cucumbers. Grateful for his narrow escape, Luca went to bed that night excited about the adventures ahead.

The next day, it was time to ride the new Vespa. But when Luca saw a huge ramp, he gulped.

Alberto pointed at him. "I know your problem. You got a Bruno in your head."

He explained that Bruno was the frightened inner voice that told him not to do things. "Luca, it's simple. Shut him up: say, 'SILENZIO, BRUNO.'"

"*Silenzio*, Bruno."

"Louder!"

"*SILENZIO, BRUNO!*"

"GOOD. Now hang on. ANDIAMOOOO!"

Before Luca could stop him, Alberto kicked off from the starting point, and the Vespa hurtled down the hill. Luca held on for dear life and closed his eyes.

"*Silenzio* Bruno *silenzio* Bruno *silenzio* Bruno SILENZIO BRUNOOOOOOOOOO—"

When he opened his eyes, the Vespa was soaring over the surface of the water. Then down they went, laughing and cheering until— *SPLASH!*

Luca rushed home that night, feeling victorious, but there he found an unpleasant surprise. His uncle Ugo, as strange as he was strange-looking, was waiting for him. Concerned about Luca's safety, his parents had decided to send him to the deep ocean to live with his uncle for the season. Luca's heart sank. If he went to the deep, it would mean the end of Alberto and of Vespas and of any chance of seeing the rest of the surface world. He made a decision. When he went to his room to pack his things, Luca snuck out the window and swam away.

Luca arrived at Alberto's hideout, fighting back his panic. "They're sending me to the deep! To live with my weird see-through uncle! What do I do?!"

Alberto pointed across the water—to the town nestled on the other side of the bay. "Will they come looking for you over there?"

Luca could hear the voice of Bruno telling him how dangerous it would be for a sea monster to go to a human town. But Alberto's voice was just as strong. "I mean, that place must be full of Vespas. There's gotta be one for us."

Luca took a deep breath. "*Silenzio*, Bruno."

Then he jumped into the water. The boys swam as fast as they could, leaping into and out of the waves, until they arrived at the town.

The town of Portorosso was a hidden jewel of the Mediterranean, a warm and cozy fishing village bursting with life and color and sound and song. The beautiful buildings were piled together like stacks of books on an uneven shelf. The aromas of smoked fish and baked bread lingered in the air while brightly colored cones of gelato dripped neon droplets over cobblestone streets. Humans were everywhere, and at the center of the piazza was a fountain. But all this paled in comparison to . . .

. . . *a real Vespa*. Luca and Alberto were still staring at the vehicle when a kid kicked a soccer ball across their path. Luca kicked it back, accidentally knocking over the Vespa! Its owner spotted Luca and Alberto. "Out-of-towners, eh? Let me welcome you. *Benvenuti a Portorosso!*"

He went on to brag that he was Ercole Visconti, five-time winner of the Portorosso Cup. Then he told Luca he stank like a fish shop, and dragged him toward the fountain. As the water sprinkled on Luca's face, he began to transform! Luckily, before Ercole noticed, a girl on a bicycle pulling a fish cart barreled between them. "Ercole! *Basta!*"

Ercole frowned. "Spewlia's here. Wow. That's how you're training for the race?"

Giulia bristled at the nickname. "*Si cierto!* Your reign of terror is coming to an end."

Defiantly, she pulled Luca and Alberto onto the cart and pedaled away. She turned to the boys. "You know, we underdogs have to look out for each other, right?"

Luca and Alberto asked Giulia about the Portorosso Cup. She explained that it was a yearly race with three stages: swimming, cycling, and eating pasta. The prize was money—enough to buy a Vespa! That was all they needed to hear. The new friends formed a team: the Underdogs.

The only problem was the entry fee. Giulia suggested they ask her father, Massimo, at supper.

That night, while Massimo cooked, he asked Giulia if she had seen the photo of a sea monster in that day's paper. She groaned. "Everyone in Portorosso pretends to believe in sea monsters."

Massimo grunted. "Well, I'm not pretending."

Luca was so surprised that he spat water on Alberto, causing half his face to transform! Luckily, he was able to dry off beneath the table. When it was time to eat, they came up with a plan: the boys would help Massimo with his fishing business!

With the race only a few days away, the Underdogs needed to train. Giulia shoved bowl after bowl in front of Alberto. "Every year they change the pasta. You have to be ready for anything! Could be cannelloni, penne, fusilli, trofie, EVEN LASAGNE!"

Meanwhile, Luca practiced riding a bicycle while he delivered fish for Massimo. It was tougher than it looked.

Worse yet, Ercole kept making things difficult. When Giulia was practicing her swimming, Ercole splashed water on Alberto! Luca knocked him overboard to hide his transformation. Giulia didn't see anything. But Ercole did—enough to make him suspicious—until Giulia rocked his boat, knocking his precious sweater into the water. He panicked. "Insane girl! It is wool! It cannot be moistened! Ciccio, make it dry! Immediately!"

Luca was discouraged by the day's events, but Giulia still believed they could win. "Look. During school, I live with my mamma in Genova. And every summer, I come here, and everyone thinks I'm just some weird kid who doesn't belong."

When asked where Genova was, she took them up a hill and pointed at a great, gleaming metal snake. It was a train, she said, the one that went to Genova, which was also where she went to school. Over the next few days, as Luca learned more about her school, he wondered. "Is your school open to everyone?"

Alberto knew what Luca was thinking, and he became afraid that Luca might leave him. Desperately, he reminded Luca of their plan to buy a Vespa and travel the world. He yanked him onto the bicycle and sped dangerously down the hill, just like they had done on the island—only this time, Luca wasn't interested. "Alberto, stop!"

"THAT'S BRUNO TALKING!"

"NO! I'M PRETTY SURE THAT'S JUST MEEEE!"

SPLASH! They landed in the water below.

When Giulia caught up with them, they had dried off. Luca asked if they could join her at school. She was elated. Alberto was fed up. "Uhh, Giulia, your school, does it take all kinds of people? I mean, what if some of them were not human?"

Then he jumped into the water—and transformed! Giulia screamed and scrambled backward. Luca knew he should tell Giulia the truth about himself, but he was too afraid. Instead, he pointed at Alberto. "SEA MONSTER!"

Alberto was shocked. Tears filled his eyes. "Luca?"

But Giulia knew the truth. "Of all the places for sea monsters to visit—Portorosso?! Ugh, what were you guys thinking?" She decided that the race was too dangerous for them. The Underdogs were no more.

That night, Luca stared out at Alberto's fort. Getting an idea, he swam over to it and found his hideout torn apart. Even the Vespa poster was ripped off the wall, and behind it were tally marks. Alberto explained that they had started when his dad left. "I just thought that . . . maybe he'd change his mind." After he had made two hundred marks, he stopped counting. "He's better off without me. You are, too. I'm just the kid that ruins everything."

Luca frowned. "*SILENZIO, BRUNO*. That's just a dumb voice in your head."

When Alberto insisted that Luca leave, Luca agreed. "Okay, I'll go. I'll go win the race."

On the day of the Portorosso Cup, Luca went straight
to the race official, Signora Marsigliese, to make sure he
could race alone. Luckily, she agreed. Giulia arrived next
and was surprised to see Luca.

He tried to put her at ease before he ran off. "Don't worry.
I'll race on my own. You won't get in any trouble."

"But—but how are you gonna . . . I-I mean, what happens
when they . . . You can't swim!"

At the starting line, Giulia nodded to Ercole's teammate
Ciccio, whom Ercole was covering in olive oil to make him more
streamlined. Then Luca, in a diving suit, lurched up.

The swimmers took their marks. BANG! The first leg of the race was underway, but Luca was frozen at the water's edge. He closed his eyes, took a deep breath, and started walking. That was all it took. He set off across the ocean floor.

As the race went on, Giulia swam as fast as she could and got an early lead. Below her, Luca struggled with a leak in his suit and began to fall behind. Ciccio was also having trouble: the fish were finding his olive-oiled skin tasty.

Giulia was still in the lead when the swimming portion was over. She hustled to the table. By the time Luca arrived, she was already halfway through her pasta. Meanwhile, Ercole cheated by shoving noodles into the mouth of his teammate Guido. Giulia finished first, but she was wobbling as she made her way toward the bike. Luca was the last one to finish his plate. But the final leg was the bicycling leg—his best one!

One by one, Luca passed each racer, even Giulia, and took the lead—until a drop of water splashed on his hand. "Huh? No no no no." He pedaled harder, hoping to outrace the rain, but the downpour grew worse. He stopped beneath an awning at the top of the hill.

Then Alberto arrived with an umbrella! "I never shoulda let you do this alone."

Luca couldn't believe it. But in the next moment, Ercole whizzed by and aimed a savage kick at Alberto. The umbrella went flying, and Alberto landed hard. Soaked, he transformed into a sea monster.

Alberto looked at Luca. "Just stay there! You're still okay!" With that, he charged into the crowd, who were approaching with harpoons, and a net pinned him to the ground.

It was Luca's chance to escape, but he no longer wanted to. He wanted to save Alberto! Kicking his bike into gear, Luca shot out into the rain. He could feel his fingers turning to webs, his skin turning to scales, and a long, slippery tail growing out over his bicycle seat. He plunged into the crowd and hoisted Alberto onto the bicycle. As they sped away, Alberto was shocked.

"Whoa! You really *are* crazy!"

"Yeah, and I learned it from you!"

As they reached the bottom of the hill, Ercole careened into view. He raised his harpoon just as Giulia appeared, pedaling so fast that her feet were a blur. She slammed into Ercole's bicycle before he could take aim. The two bikes crashed into the sidewalk. Ercole shook his fist.

When Luca and Alberto saw Giulia on the ground, they dropped their bike and ran back to her.

The three friends stayed together, Luca standing tall in the face of Ercole and his harpoon.

To everyone's surprise, Massimo arrived. "I know who they are." He grabbed Alberto's hand and held it up. "They are the winners."

The Underdogs looked around, confused. Yet there was the bicycle, lying across the finish line. They had won! As Luca and Alberto cheered, Giulia gave them a big hug. "Yeah, we did it!"

Just then, Luca's parents rushed over. They had seen the race, and they were so proud.

Meanwhile, Ciccio and Guido got fed up with Ercole and tossed him in the fountain. "AH! Ah, ah, I can't swim! Ah, ah, oh!"

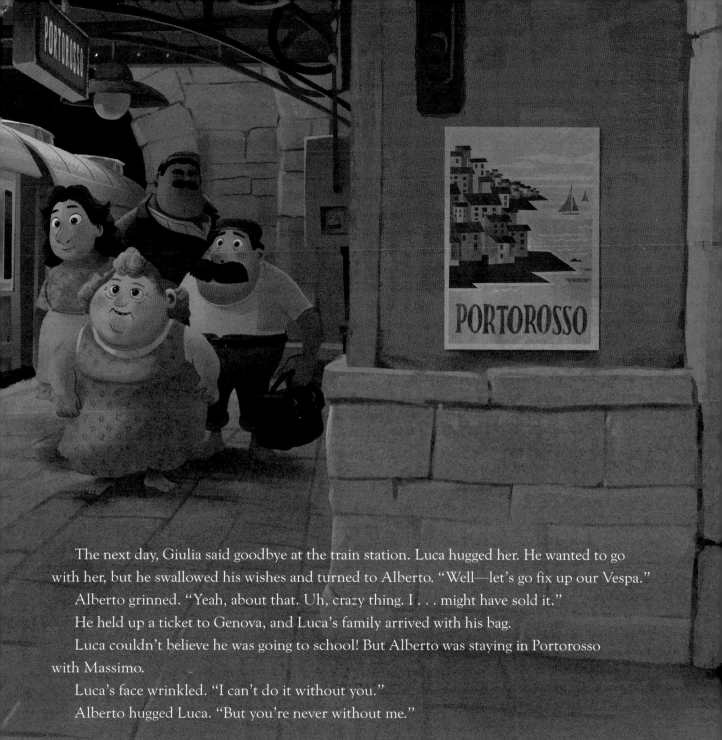

The next day, Giulia said goodbye at the train station. Luca hugged her. He wanted to go with her, but he swallowed his wishes and turned to Alberto. "Well—let's go fix up our Vespa."

Alberto grinned. "Yeah, about that. Uh, crazy thing. I . . . might have sold it."

He held up a ticket to Genova, and Luca's family arrived with his bag.

Luca couldn't believe he was going to school! But Alberto was staying in Portorosso with Massimo.

Luca's face wrinkled. "I can't do it without you."

Alberto hugged Luca. "But you're never without me."

As the train chugged through the countryside, Luca looked ahead. The entire world was at his feet—like a great map stretching out before him with all kinds of mysteries and adventures hidden in its folds. He couldn't wait to explore every bit of it.

Andiamo. Here we go!